# THAT ONE GIRL

## WHEN LOVE BECOMES ILLUSION.

ABINASH MAHAPATRA

*It is with genuine gratitude and warm regard that I dedicate this book of mine wholeheartedly to my beloved parents, who have been my source of inspiration and gave me strength throughout till the accomplishment of the task.*

# Contents

# Contents

# About The Author

Abinash Mahapatra is born in Odisha and has done his schooling from St. Xavier's High School, Puri. He is currently pursuing B.tech in Electrical Engineering from GITA Autonomous College, Bhubaneswar.

He has experience of publishing article in the esteemed newspaper "Orissa Times " and had been Co-author to many Anthologies. He has keen interest in reading Novels and Playing chess. He aspires to utilize his skills in the field of writing creating a great difference. "THAT ONE GIRL (When Love becomes Illusion)" is his debut novel.

He can be contacted at : imabinash028x@gmail.com

You can find his exclusive poetry and quote at : @___.the_words.___

His Instagram ID: @am_abinash.___

# Acknowledgements

History of all great work into witness that no great work has ever been done without either active or passive support of a person's surrounding and one's close quarter. I am overwhelmed and grateful to acknowledge my deepest thanks to my mentor and friend **Subhrajeet Harichandan**, whose immense support had made this work of mine came into existence.

I would like to extend my deepest gratitude to my bestie **Saswati Priyadarshini Das.** Her relentless support, trust over me, motivation and some times as a critics had played a great role in shaping this story of mine into greater perfection. Without her words of motivation, I could have never been enable to muster up courage to take on this task.

I owe my special thanks to my senior Sugiani Di and Radhasmita Di for constantly showing their support and love for me. The worthy experience shared by my sister Barsha, Swagatika , and two of my bestie Preeti and Swarupa had helped me a lot throughout this work of mine to stay motivated and have a believe on myself despite the situation of hopelessness.

I thank to all my fellow friends: Biswajeet, B.Ganesh, Swayankar , Ashish, Ansuman, Ankita, Kausar, Suryaprakash, Suryakanta, Ananya, Sambit and to all my beloved sisters for their worthy support. Their constant love, motivation, care for me and kept me enthusiast towards my task.

Lastly but not the least, I would be thankful before Almighty God for keeping my blessed with power of mind, protection and skill , healthy life. Without these blessings I had never be the one, What I am Today.

# Preface

***"Love is an endless mystery, for it has nothing else to explain it."***

This wonderful line by the Nobel Laureate Rabindranath Tagore had explained the depth of the emotion LOVE, and this line somehow greatly connects to the story of this book. As mentioned above, Love is a mystery that may take time upto infinite period to get understood. We try to explain and express it in our own way, but everytime it come up with a new phase to be explored with.

Here in this book, Bhavesh describes the story of his past love before his wife Arushi. It didn't began all of a sudden. Everyday he had a practice of writing few pages in his diary before going to sleep. That stormy night while his wife was slept early, his sobbing voice broke through her ears. While she woke up, she was shocked to see his eyes full of tears while he was holding a beautiful portrait of her. On asking him the reason, the reply had just filled her heart with sorrow and condolence for the past that he had gone through.

Let's explore the story hidden behind his words that left the heart of Arushi filled up with sympathy for Bhavesh's past. I feel all the readers will appreciate the cause behind and will surely get the feel of Love being called the "Endless Mystery".

Wish you all a Happy Reading......

# LOVE: BEAUTIFUL EMOTION WITH BITTER TRUTH ‼

*"When looking into their eyes*
*Makes you read their heart,*
*When opening without the lips*
*You read their unsaid Pain,*
*Then that is what you define the divine love as."*

The Philosophical interpretation of LOVE can never be completely accurate. It is just like assuming the steps of the players in the chess without having Zero idea about it's rule. The more effort we put in to explain it accurately, the dense we get trapped into it. Yeh, Love is never a trap. It allows you to set yourself free from the limitations. Once it become adulterated with feelings like expectations, beauty and lust, then from the next moment only it begins to loose it's sanity. Hence sometimes Love becomes a viscous trap too.

Sometime we come across the situation in life where we have to choose either between our love or our responsibilities. In this Materialistic World, nothing could be more terrible situation than this that one could go through. In this case, we have to prioritize the responsibility over love. Love never teaches us to be coward. It always give lesson of sacrifices and strengthen us to take on the challenges of life. Some may get wondered with this fact, but yes it does lays much beyond expressing love with just words or gifts. Its sometime present in between the sternness of a person. Like the Neem had greater positive effect on the body but still tastes quite bitter. The same goes for the Love. Not always you can expect the result you wish for. They bear fruit only as destined by the time. Making effort to achieve your love is no harm until when you are believer in the Power of Acceptance for the truth.

"I mayn't be the smile over your face, but still I wish that may your grinning face charm everyday much better than the yesterday."

***This interpretation to the emotion Love had never been such strong to be elongated before you without the wonderful words of motivation by my bestie Ms. Swarupa Mishra. I greatly thank her for making me gain the trust over the supremacy of love back again when I was struggling each moment to move on from my past heartbreaks. I'm just blessed to a bestie like you in my life.***

# I

# The Romantic Evening

It was raining hard that evening. Suddenly there occurred power flickering after a huge thundering sound. During the month of November, this kind of weather was completely brisk. Despite this severe weather outside, the slamming sound of utensils from the kitchen break through the pleasant silence in the gallery. Even the screaming voice was heard too. Bhavesh was then sitting in the porch and enjoying the weather outside. On hearing such strange noise, he switched on the flashlight in the phone and rushed towards the kitchen. What he saw the moment next had left his mouth wide-opened. The sight has just made his heart quivered.

"What have you done to yourself bae!" He yelled with agony.

He hurriedly rushed into and caressingly hold her bleeding hand due to sharp cut. To the coincidence, the power has come back on. He managed to bring her out of the kitchen and took her to the drawing room, making her sit over the couch. Tears were continually rolling down her eyes out of pain. Soon he found the First-Aid box and managed successfully to stop the bleeding by applying salve on it. This had brought some relief to her and he wiped-out tears over her cheek. She adoringly hugged him.

"How did it all happened ?" He asked. "You know how terrified I was, to see your hands bleeding such drastically." He uttered the lines with tearful eyes and numbing lips.

She grinned and replied, "hey it was nothing like that serious dear. I was infact startled by the large thundering sound and by mistakenly cut my hand while chopping the vegetables."

" We will arrange something for dinner from outside tonight, Don't worry !" He said. "You better have some rest over here I'm just coming," and then he left.

After few time, he came with some fries and cup of tea. While she was busy in scrolling down her phone, his voice had interrupted her mind and she was just amazed. "Arey yaar kya zarurat thi in sabki!!" And she chuckled.

"Let's walk into the stoop and enjoy the weather outside. Hope you will enjoy snacks prepared by me." "Will try it for sure then..." and moved into the gallery. They enjoyed the evening over there and time passed by. Within this time, Arushi was felt asleep over the shoulder of Bhavesh after some talk. It was striking around 19:00PM over the clock. He awakened her. With traces of laziness over her eye she asked, " kya hua yaar ? Itna pleasant mausam phir kahan milta hai". He laughed a bit on hearing such.

"I think we had to have our dinner from outside tonight," he uttered.

"Oh yeh!!" She exclaimed.

Both of them got ready and went to the Avenue Restaurant near by their apartment. The aroma of the grass was just pleasant and the cool breeze that was blowing was completely making each of the moment damn romantic. Avenue Restaurant was well known for its Open Sky Dinning Service across the Noida. Both of them had a finger licking dinner. A plate of Sahi Panner and Tandoori had just made their day complete. While walking down the street back to home, she asked, "when mama and papa are going to return ?" "Probably this week, they are going to return from Pilgrimage." Soon they reached to their home back.

They got freshen and prepared the bedsheet for sleep. Every night, Bhavesh had a habit of writing diary before going to sleep. The same was there for that day. She then slept and he was busy in his writing. After sometime She heard the sobbing voice which had made her awaken. She was shocked to see his eyes full of tear while he was holding a beautiful portrait of her. In a sympathetic voice she asked, "what's wrong dear ?" What she saw the moment next had just puzzled her mind......

# II

# It's hard to imagine life without YOU

He was amazed to see her waking up. Hastily he wipe away the tears over his cheeks and put on the smile so as to hide his emotion. All that was in vain. She had already caught sight of it.

“Why are you sobbing!” She exclaimed.

He just giggled. “Hey there’s nothing infact something had just dropped onto my eyes.”

“I don’t think so,” she replied in seriousness. “I know you are pretending to act fine, but you aren’t. If it’s true that you are okay then why the pages of your diary doesn’t depict so.” She hold the wet pages of the diary and asked him.

He just remained dumbfounded. She found out the portrait of her which was nicely drawn by him. She exclaimed, “ Ahh you draw so nice! Why were you then trying to hide it from me.” Actually, I wanted to keep it secret as of now and present it as a surprise on your Birthday." Her glittering eyes had expressed the happiness she was holding in her heart after hearing this from him. "Yeh that's so nice of you yaar." "You know na how much I love surprise" , she blushed.

"Everytime you present me something is damn special, memorable and lovely for me. But wait a second, the tears I found over your eyes was not out of any other reason except sadness. Don't try to lie me. So, am I right ? And if yes, then why!!!" She yelled.

"Hehe..." He chuckled. "The way you're getting that serious is not the reason as you are feeling. You know, I was just whimpering imagining what would be my life had been without you. Even a single moment it's hard to imagine my life without you. Your presence matters a lot to me." He hold her lacerated hands caressingly and said, " You know how distraught I was when I found such gashing marks over your hand".

"Tum itne senti maat bano yaar", She exclaimed. "I had never felt you getting such emotional ever before. My heart just got exuded. Now no tears please. Tell me honestly, what had happened to you. May be we both can together fine solution to it."

"Are you really that serious ? " He asked.

"Of course, why not !" She exclaimed.

"Actually I want to share the painful yet desirable memories that I have been holding on in my heart for you. The past had done me something so worst that still it's memory make me terrified of loosing you in my life. I hope you won't judge me," he said.

"Hey dear, have you ever felt such from me. Just free yourself from the cage of past and set yourself into the free sky of the present. That's all what I want," she said.

"So, I was telling......."

# III

# Those Magical Eyes

"Ahh...."He just mustered up. "Where should I start from! Even I can't understand."

She had perceived his discomfit state and his nervousness for recalling his memories. The traces of emotional fluctuation going through his mind was clearly visible through his eyes. She patted her back. "Hey! Are you here or not ?" She asked.

He just got startled. "Yeh I'm sorry," he exclaimed.

Before he could take on his story ahead, she jumped into his words. " Listen......listen," she uttered. "Before you share anything let me make some points clear. Before we tied our knot, we were best friends and yes we are still. As we had never been shy of sharing each other problem, so why today! I have enough trust on you and I'm never going to judge you too. Now you can continue." She then grinned. "Can I continue then without hesitation?" He asked. "Of course, What are you waiting for!" She exclaimed. "I am very happy that you made me feel relaxed and comfortable. Perhaps, now I can expound my story before you and I feel this will make you realize the cause behind my shredded tears." With a very heavy voice, he started......

"I was then studying in Delhi Public School, Noida. Like you know Arushi, Students of DPS had different level of viewpoint and approach towards any situation. Especially we boys were more confounded rather than girls," he chuckled. "I clearly remember the day when I was in class 08 and the month was perhaps of October. Our Mathematics lecture was then overed by 14:55PM. The bell had rung and it could clearly be recalled the withered face of each and everyone of my class. "Ek to math ka session dimag kha rakha tha aur upar sey last mey rakhe they bachon ka favorite period", He reminisced and laughed. Tell me Aru, "Tumhare najariye mey sabse interesting period konsa walla tha... hehee", he asked mockingly. She thought for a while and replied : "Umm... ,I guess it's the PT Period." Both of them laughed out a lot on this reaction.

"Hey! Now let's move on... .(He continued)

All the students were then assembled over the field. When suddenly a harsh voice had cracked through the microphone that made the howling voice of crowd into pin drop silence. Aur woh 220 V ki madhur awaj hamare respected PT sir ka tha," he grinned. "Hey Bhagwan !" She exclaimed. "You boys had literally a very bad practice of making mock over someone and especially when it comes to PT sir. Matlab janmo ki dushmani hoti hai kya ! And she laughed out a lot. "Arey yaar.......", He chuckled. "I am not like them about whom you are saying. It's actually was the trend in our school days ...hehee....."

"Soon Our PT session was started. We have done the exercises as instructed . After few moments my eyes suddenly met with a girl who was standing beside to me in the opposite row. It was like the first time my eyes had encountered with any girl in a different manner." He blushed while saying this line.

(Awkward silence was there)

"Arey agey ka bologey ya ushka kuch tax lagega... ", She taunted.

"Hmm... soon within few moments Our PT class was over. I was really like out of my mind and had weak concentration over the period. It was literally getting burden over me, and I decided to express the situation before my bestie. When I returned to the class to take my bag, I had then explained all these to Siddharth, one of my bestie. What he replied next had just ignited my anxiety to another level......"

"Hmmmmm........." ,She murmured.

"Kya yaar tum bhi..." He blushed.

# IV

# Sometimes waiting is the hardest thing of All

"Arey tum ushke barey mey bata rahe ho."
"Hmm....."
"She is actually one of my friend's cousin sister. Well bhai tu tension mat le. I will let you inform more detail about her soon. Bas patience rakho. Mey hun na", Siddharth said. These lines made me feel more comfortable but still filled me up with higher level of anxiety.

That evening I returned home with heart filled with anxiousness, craziness etc. The situation was like, as if my adernaline had stopped being secreted and I was battling with higher level of uncomfortability. My facial expression was clearly depicting the situation I was going through. Even when I returned home mama had noticed it. She enquired, "Kya hua beta is there any specific problem?" And

I denied. I got refreshed, had my lunch and went to have rest. Back in the evening when I got back to my study table, I was packed with considerable no. of assignment. But my heart was not letting my mind to get myself free from the moment I had gone through in the PT period.

You know I could recall a line, "jab ham kisi bakt ke jald guzzar jane ki intezar karte hai tab mano bakt ki rafter thamsi jati hai".

Something was like that going on my life. My eagerness to know her was getting higher each and every moment passing by. I was experiencing the greatest level of uncomfortability. Even that night, I was unable to sleep.

"Ek baat bolun.....", He asked.

"Yup, carry on...." Arushi replied with great eagerness.

I would like to recollect the line, "Jab ap kisi chit ki intezaar besabri sey karte hai to bakt apki sabr ki pariksha leti hai." He said. "Yeh baat to sahi hai", she replied.

"My life was going through that stage, when I was struggling with my anxiety and still expecting the right time as I was left with no other option. Infact, the very next day was Sunday. Usually on Sunday, I used to go out to play with my friends. But this time the scenario was something different. As I slept late in the night, hence I woke up late in the morning. I got refreshed and had my breakfast. It was around 10:00AM in the morning. All my colony mates were assembled at the near by playground. On the normal weekend, I used to reach the field earlier than other . Unfortunately the traumatic situation was bothering my mind. Even some of my friend had came to call up me. I denied. I was really stuck in the assignment for the whole day. Late in the evening , I went for a walk . Down the streets the scenario of nature was fascinating. Rather enjoying it , I was wishing her to be with me." He grinned.

Arushi while listening the story was completely reddened with both jealous and his level of childness. He then managed to pacify her feelings. "Hey... tum bura maat mano yar. If I will not open up these secrets of my life then things are going to be damn difficult to be cracked" He said in a gentle voice. "Arey yaar.... Worry not dear, I am not going to judge you ever", She replied.

(He then continued story ahead)
Any how I was able to manage the weekend by making myself engaged in the stuffs I was left with to complete. I was eagerly waiting for the rising Sun on Monday. Early in the Morning I woke up with great refreshment. My level of enthusiasm was in it's zenith. I got ready for the school and reached the stop at time. My friend Sushan had noticed that delighted smile over my face.
He asked, "Kya baat hai bhai...Aj itne khus kyu dikh rahe ho ...Kuch to gadbad hai...".
"Arey yaar kya tum subha subha suru hogaye. Nothing much special dear", I replied.
"Hmm...Sab to sirf Siddharth ko bataogey ham hote kon hai", Sushan mocked.
When I reached at the School, my heart was like beating more faster. I don't know why...But it was . Our assembly was over and we came back to class. On seeing Siddharth, I was elated. "Kahan reh gaya tha bhai...Badi intezzar tumhari kar raha tha..", I yelled.
"Control bhai....itna utawla mat bano", He replied with laugh.
"Arey bhai Saturday sey to control rakhe hai", I replied.
I: "Did you asked your friend about her?"
Siddharth: "Yeh... I asked. Her name is SHRADHANJALI MISRA. She is from Class 07 B."

I: "Thanks a lot bhai...Well did you have any more information about her?"
Siddharth: "Hmm. My friend Anup is her cousin. He was saying, She is a bright student and had topped many competitive exam. Apart from it, She is a good Sports person. She had been part to state level Gymnastics and is currently selected for National Level. He hadn't mention anything about her love affairs issue."
I: "Ahh... I could remember her face now easily. Woh to wahi hai sayad , jise hamare VP ma'am felicitate kiye they last week."
Siddharth: "Hmm. Last week she had qualified the state level Gymnastic."
I: "I am damn happy yaar. I don't know how to express my gratitude for this help of yours."
Siddharth: "Hogaya tumhara to nikal lo..." (And he laughed)
During the break period, I had went near the Class 07 B. I couldn't find her on a sudden. I then waited there for a while with sid. He was bit impatient to get back to class for completing his assignments. Finally, after waiting for five minutes that pretty face had took away my heart once again. My step had just started swinging. My exultancy was noticed by many. Siddharth had just pulled my hands back with great force. "Bhai tumhari excitement kuch jyada badh rahi hai. Yaha sey nikal le nhi to tumhare wajah sey donos ko musibat mol leni padegi", He said. I then went back to my class.
I couldn't explain the happiness that I went through while my second time encounter with Shradhanjali. I couldn't believe that my period of patience was over. Late in the evening when I reached back at my stoppage. Sushan shouted out, "MISRAJI...Hmmm".
I was Startled to hear this. Before I could ask him anything,

his papa had arrived to pick him up from the stoppage.

# V

# Finally, it really happened

That line said by Sushan was disturbing my mind throughout the evening. Yeh, I was not much disturbed like the evening of Saturday. But yes, Somehow I was unable to cope up with my studies. I was bit insecured. Actually, I never like to disclose my relationship issue to anyone except my close one's. I couldn't trace any such moment where I could find Sushan, near me and Siddharth while discussing about Shradhanjali. I was completely perplexed with what was going on.

Next day when I met with him at the stoppage I asked him, "Arey yaar kal jate bakt itna jor sey MISRAJI karke kisse sey bulaye". Sushan replied, "Nhi woh mera ek colony ka dost us bakt hamara stoppage sey hokar ja raha tha". His reply had perhaps relieved my fast beating nerves. We then went to school. Like the first day, it had now became the habit of mine to roam near class 07 B during the break hour. Baat to nhi ho pati thi but woh hota hai na dur sey dekh kar dil khus karlena. It was going something like that with me. Some of my friends had noticed these for certain days and finally, they asked me. One day, I was sitting ideal in a corner in the class as sid was absent. Yess, days were tough in school without best friends. Class me kuch karne me maja hin nahi aata unke bina.

"Well Aru... how were school days?" Bhavesh asked.

Arushi: Honestly bolu then... I don't have such problems like you actually. Agar meri bestie Shittal ati thi to bhi thik and if due to any reason she was absent then I had back up option with other classmates.

Bhavesh: Chalo yeh baat bhi sahi hai.

(Both of them giggled)

(He then continued his story......)

I was sitting ideal in my seat, while Sushan sat beside me. "Ky hua yaar. Aj Sid nhi aya to kya din khali khali lag raha hai na!!!" He said. I replied with nodding my head. Suddenly, during that time Shradhanjali came to my class. I went crazy with joy. Sushan had marked my expression . Shradhanjali had actually came along with her friend. Her friend was having birthday that day.

Later when she went back Sushan asked, "Kya bhai crush hai tumhari. Ussey dekhne ke baad pura happy happy....".

I just chuckled.

"Kya yaar tum bhi.. kabhi kahi bhi suru ho jate ho. Matlab kuch bhi....",I replied.

Sushan: "If you don't mind bruh. I had seen you being changed a bit from the past days."

I: "I didn't get you. You mean I had changed. How!!!"

Sushan: "Hmm Ajakal to tum class mey break period mey sirf upper floor ko chale jate ho. Kuch sey to sunna bhi hai ki tumhari class 07 ke kisi ladki par crush agaya hai."

I preferred to remain silence.

When Siddharth had attended the class next day, I asked him about Sushan. He replied that he was unaware of all those. Even he was shocked to hear this. My tension has then increased by then. I could realise that someone was keeping an eye on me. Well I don't have enmity with anyone, but still there were some students in the class who were jealous of me. I don't have idea about why does they do so. The days gradually went on. Our exam was approaching nearer. It was the month of February and we were to appear our final Summative Assessment Examination. Probably, I was prepared by then. On the examination day, I hadn't expected a grand surprise from lord to my expectation.

(Arushi interrupted with a question)

Arushi: Itni khusi ki kya baat thi. Usi din propose kardiya kya!!!

Bhavesh: Nope yaar. I hadn't done such stuff that day. Have patience I am telling na.

(He continued then again.....)

While entering my exam hall, the scene had just made my eyes wide opened. My heart just pounded with joy. Exact to my front was sitting Shradhanjali. To the corner of the room Sid was there. He just gave me wink. I was literally dumbstruck in my elation. I sat behind her. The exam was started then. I had successfully completed the paper in time and was sitting ideal. Shradhanjali was facing certain problems in the question. She had asked her friend who was sitting beside me. When she was unable to help out her, She asked me. My voice had just been numbed. On hearing her voice for the first time it went deep into the heart. I had managed to conceal my expression from her and helped her out. When the paper was over, she thanked me for the help.

Siddharth then came near me.

Siddharth: Hey Shradhanjali!

Shradhanjali: Bhai how did you knew my name!

Siddharth: Well tum Anup Sharma from KV ushke cousin ho right? Umm he is from class 08.

Shradhanjali: Hmmmmm.

Siddharth: Ahh... He is my friend actually.

(Shradhanjali blushed)

Siddharth then made my introduction with her. She was really very nice person. From the first day, I could feel the friendship she shared. Before leaving , she shaked hands with me. In return I wished her for the best performance in the upcoming exams.

This opportunity had really paved my path of friendship with her. I thanked lord for this opportunity. All that was going to happen the next moment was filled with joy. I was really feeling blessed.

# VI

# Wished this moment would've paused

Arushi: Bhavesh, still I couldn't relate any cause that made you cry before few time.

Bhavesh: Don't be impatient. I am sure after knowing the reason your curious heart will not be insatiate anymore that you are feeling right now.

(He continued the story then....)

Time passed. Our examination was over and we were on a holiday till the results were out. During these period, my heart missed her presence. I felt addicted to her. While the examination was going on, we had many conversations. It made my bonding with her up to a great level. Whatever numbers of day that I had spend with her was like a memory.

It was the month of March. Our results were declared. Hopefully I secured 90.5%. It was although not much in comparison to my classmates grades. Still I was happy with it. That evening Siddharth had came to meet me at my home. We both had enough of amusements. It included various indoor games and random talks. I asked him about Shradhanjali.

Siddharth: She had secured around 96.85%. Sunna to yeh bhi hai ki she had shared the first positon of her class with another classmate of her named “Deepak”.

His words just made me felt happy for her. I asked him about when the school was going to open. He replied that the school was going to reopen from the first of the April. And the day in the present was around mid of the month (March). Like the initial days, I had to once again hold on patience with me. I await for the day.

Finally, the period of anticipation came to an end. It was first of April. I went to school with mind filled with refreshment and happiness. I was more curious of the new lessons that were going to be started then. To my surprise her section class 08 A was just in front of my class. On the first day when she met with me, she greeted with me thanks. At first I was bit dumbfounded to reply her. Then she resuscitated me by her hands moving over my eyes. “Sry sry...I was bit confused. Well I couldn’t get you”, I said. She replied: I wouldn’t have been topper of my class without your help. I just chuckled and said, “Hey its nothing like that dear. You made the things possible. I’m no one to make you enable for so.” She just once again thanked me and left away.

Gradually with course of time we had built up close acquaintances. Everyday we began to meet each other during the break time. We shared the tiffin too. Many a time, she used to go with me to walk around the park in the school. Many of our teachers objected the level of friendship we shared. The things became so intense when one of our teacher caught me sharing my whole lunch with her. The matter reached up to our home. Fortunately ,both of our parents exhibited higher level of understanding and didn't judge us. They just simply made us understand the scenario going over in the teen days just to make us aware of the life situation, going besides of many. Yeh it's not like that they supported our friendship but hmm they didn't even scolded us for it too. Soon the things became normal. We had our summer holiday of 45 days. I t was really a very long period of time. I scared that if she would forget me. Every morning my mind makes me remember of her presence with me. I was not present with her but still I was making my heart understood the cause of it. Somehow the time went on. From that incident of Case like both of our family became family friends.

Before the things would become a burden, the school opened. Classes begun to run normally. As I was in class 09, I was bit stucked in the study more than her. We still make out time to take the note of each other's health, study and life.

One day we had planned to go out for a trip. Our location was fixed for Okhla Bird Sanctuary, Noida. It was the month of September and the traces of Cold weather had just begin. The chilling winds blowing across the road in the morning was remarking the advent of winter. It was like a damn romantic environment.

We both were done with all our left over assignments. On a weekend, we had informed our parents that we were going on a group trips with our friend. Initially her parents didn't agree to let her go. But one of her friend Radhika made them convinced of the fact. Really, there are some who are never into love but still values the feeling of it.

Perhaps Radhika, was one among them. We planned to meet at @09:30AM. We met at the point as decided earlier and hired an auto. We had a pleasant day over there. The natural scenario had just made each and every moment filled with ample of memories. We both were so friendly that non can notice us that we share the age difference.

Shradhanjali: Well you had been friend of mine for around 06 months. How do u feel about me ?

I: To be honest, I had never met such a friendly person. Yeh I do have friends like Siddharth but when it comes to girl, no one had ever been so close friend of mine. Well can I ask you a question.

Shradhanjali: Yeh... you can.

I: What made you choose me as your friend. I know there are many who are like mad after you. But non among them you give much value. Then why it's me.

Shradhanjali: Mmmmm ... I hadn't ever thought of such reasons. All I know is that I feel comfortable around you. Yeh you're elder to me but had never let me felt that. Rather you choose to be a good friend of mine. And hmm the most wonderful side I found within you is the care and support you give me. I can never forget the favor you did to me during the examination.

(I just grinned and felt goosebumps)

I: Well its enough yaar. Aur kitne baar thank you bologey for this. Hehheee.

We had got certain snaps over there. It was striking around @03:00PM over the clock. Soon we found a good restaurant near by. We then had our lunch.

The very next day She had to leave for the national level gymnastics competition, going to be held at Pune. For her shopping of the accessories required for the trip and sports , we went to the DLF Mall of India. There we done the shopping and as it was evening by then so we had also some snacks at KFC. By around @05:45PM I dropped her nearby her home. I wished her for giving the best in the competition.

This time she had to remain absent for around 15 days for the competition. It was hard to see off herself but I had to.......

# VII

# The moment that made HER feel special

The very next day she departed for the competition to be held at Pune. She had her train 1105x JHELUM EXPRESS in the morning at around @09:45AM. Perhaps it was only her bestie Radhika and me who missed her presence a lot in the school. Yeh, those days Siddharth beared company with me. Whenever I felt the absence of her and pushed my mind into sadness, he came forward with a helping hand to support me. I could really feel the line "*A friend in need is a friend indeed.*" If during those days he wouldn't have been with me then I would have lost my confidence. As I was not having cell phone of mine, I wasn't able to keep track about her health and all. Everyday on the way while coming to the school I came across the temple. I could remember that I used to pray for her happiness and healthy life before Lord Shivji. Those fifteen days were like any fifteen etymology for me.

Yeh soon those fifteen days passed by. Finally one day, while stepping down from the bus in the morning, I came across that one face for whom I was longing for the last fortnight. I felt that shining eyes which was depicting her decisive victory in the competition. Soon that day in the assembly, she was felicitated over the stage by Principal ma'am. Those of echo of applause was like making my heart filled with rejoice. Back in the lunch period she met me.

Shradhanjali: Hey ! How are u... Abhi tak congrats tak bhi nhi bola apne.

I: Arey esi baat nhi hai yaar. Mai to bahut happy hoon that you had achieved such great by becoming second in the national level.

Shradhanjali: Well, I was saying that I had arranged one party in evening at "*THE PATIALA KITCHEN*". *I would request you to join in please.*

*I: Sure. Don't need to say please.....Ek baar tumne bulaya means hamara ana pakka.*

*(She just blushed and went away.)*

*Later that evening many of her friends Radhika, Gourav, Somesh, Shima, Heena, Uday etc. & I reached there . We had a grand celebration. She offered us Cake, Burger and some other snacks. When the party was over and everyone left, I presented her a gift. She was just shocked. She couldn't think what for it was.*

*Shradhanjali: What's this for!*

*I: You gave us such a wonderful party and preferred to enjoy your victory with us. It now becomes obligation to present you something for making you feel special.*

*(Tear just rolled down her eyes in happiness.)*

*Shradhanjali: Just love you dear. It's a sense of happiness for me. I hadn't ever felt that someone feel more special about it me.*

*I was expecting it from Radhika but she didn't.*

*I: It's okie. Don't act pessimistic now. I'm there na. I would request to open up the gift.*

*(She opened up the wrapper. In the first box there was a waterproof workout smart watch and in the second gift there was a small statue of Lord Shivji. She was damn happy but still confused.)*

*Shradhanjali: Yeh watch tak thik tha but I couldn't get the cause behind the murti.*

*I: I had presented it to you as the mark of health. I wish everyday your strength would get increased and may his blessings be with you forever. I feel it's already getting late. We should leave now.*

*I then dropped her at her home. The things were going normal like usual.*

*One evening, I was sitting in the porch of my apartment. Suddenly the door bell ranged. While I opened the door, I was just numb with amazement. Before my eyes were Parents of Shradhanjali and along with them was Siddharth.*

# VIII

# The wait was almost Over !!!

On seeing Shradhanjali's parents in the horrified condition I was bit stunned. I couldn't understand what was going on. Before her parents could say anything, Siddharth spoke out.

Siddharth: Hey! Please come with us Bhavesh. Please don't make any delay , else today there will extinguish the lamp of life .

Suddenly my mama came from the kitchen after hearing the desperate voice of Siddharth. More of being happy, she got amazed on seeing Shradhanjali's parents being in tensed state. At first she scolded me, "Ab tumne fir koi nayi problem kar diya kiya. Samjhaya tha utna uss din na". My mind was completely puzzled and I felt dizzy. Fortunately her mama had took myside.

Shradhanjali's Mama: Usey mat dantiye. Usne kuch nhi kiya hai. Hame please usey hamare sath jane ki permission dijiye.

My Mama: Arey par hua to kya bataiye.

Her Mama: Shradhanjali had met with accident and no where we are getting 0 -ve blood. Siddharth told us that Bhavesh had 0 -ve blood. Please save her.

On hearing this from her, my body just started to shiver. I couldn't believe on my ear. Without any delay mama allowed me to leave with them. Soon we drove to the "Felix Hospital". I was taken to the blood donation chamber. After filling up certain medical formalities, I donated around 350ml blood. I was then asked to take some rest. When I opened my eyes after a nap, I found her parents hugging me with eyes full of tear. I was literally startled.

Her Mama: We will never forget this help of yours. You are like any blessing to her life.

I: No aunty, It's not that. Its my duty to help her.

I then went back to home with a heavy heart. I couldn't express what state of sorrow and pain I was going through that moment. All I wanted is to remain silence and captivate myself in a room. I was not depressed, but I was sad with all that incident. I prayed for her soon recovery at the nearby Temple of my home. I longed for the response from either her parents or she herself everyday. It took around a time of a week and half. One evening Siddharth came to my home.

Siddharth: Thank God yaar, She is okie now.

(On hearing this line from him, I hugged him.)

I: Next to lord , I will always remain thankful to you for making me realize the importance of mine in her life.

The very next day, Shradhanjali came to school. I was happy to see her getting recovered. As it was the class time so I couldn't interacted with her. Later during the recess time, I met with her.

I: Hey! Kaise ho yaar .... How did it all happened. Are you feeling okie now?

She: Yeh. (Tears in her eyes)

I: Arey kya hua... All fine na! Why are you crying yaar?

She: I don't know how to be thanked for this great help for yours. That day you had gifted me the Statues of Lord Shivji. Probably if that day I wouldn't have kept that with me then its sure that I would never have come back alive.

I: Hey.....Control yaar. There is nothing special of mine. Lord had saved your life. I had just given my small contribution in his work. And yes I'm happy for it.

Our break bell ranged.

Later that evening, her parents came along with her to my home. They thanked me and my parents for this great help. Even they invited us to there home for the dinner one day. After a long series of talks, my mama got agreed for it. So on their request, we went to their home. We had dinner over there. That evening was wonderful with her. I had never expected that we would become so nice friends one day and things are going to be so smooth. It was really a great pleasure for me to spend time with her at her home.

Gradually time passed by. We then had our final exams. She was bit weak that time in her studies due to medical treatment. I helped her out in completing the courses in time. Hopefully, she was able to keep track of all the lessons taught and put all her efforts to give the best. When did One year passed before the eyes I couldn't feel it also. On the first day of the examination, I recollected the memory in alone when I first met with her and the day where our friendship had started a year back.

But one thing that I noticed within her, she was more coughing those days after the treatment. One day even she had blood vomit. I was terrified but soon it was proofed that it was not that much serious and she was cured.

She had now been a good friend of mine, we both had spent many good times together and at many points she had made me felt my special value in her life.

I decided one day........

# IX

# The thing I was really afraid of!

It was from my class 08 days, when I fell in love with her. I had never dared to express my feelings before her. All I remained, the way she wanted me to be with her. Soon did two year passed through and I was then in class 10 and still I was holding on the feeling in my heart. Yeh it was somehow choking my mind at times but still I had never that courage to express it before her. Actually I was bit terrified about, if I would express and things begin to ruin between her and me. Besides these dilemma running on my mind, I decided one day to propose her.

It was the month of July. Both of us were on trip to a mall for shopping. After the incident of her accident, Our family had now relied on the level of friendship we both shared. After our shopping was done, I asked her to have some snacks in the street side restaurant and then get back to home. That evening was bit cloudy weather. Chilling wind was blowing through and I could feel the essence of love in my heart for her. We then had A cup of Tea and some fried Pakode. She was really happy to have it. I hadn't expected that it was going to be the last smiling face that I would be able to see ever in my life. As soon as our snacks were finished, I asked her to wait for a minute.

To her astonishment I gave her a chocolate . She was shocked.

She: Is there something special !

I: No. Can't I get my friend a chocolate. Do I always need any special occasion to present something to you.

(She grinned)

She: Definitely no.... Hehhee

I: Hey! I actually want to say you one thing.

She: Go ahead.

(She could notice the uncomfortable mind and terrified eyes of mine. She then made me feel relaxed)

She: Don't worry. We are good friends right. Why are you then feeling shy to express your thing before me. Have I ever felt such to share any story of mine before you.

I: Na... I didn't mean such actually.

She: Okie fine. Don't worry open up your mind. I'm all ear.

I: Actually from the last two years I had been waiting for this moment.

She: For today!!

I: Yeh, I mean for the moment when I could tell one reality of my life.

She: See you are igniting my eagerness. Now are you going to tell or I'm going to leave.

I: No please don't mind. Actually, I' m in love with you. You had meant this to me from the last two years but I had never dared to express it before you in scare of loosing you from my life.

(She just laughed with serious mood. I was bit shocked on

such reaction of her.)
I: Kya hua. I am bit confused yaar.
She: Well you cracked a nice joke now. If I'm not wrong then!
I: NO. Its true in fact.
She: Well let me clear one thing don't expect anything from me like this. We are good friends and will be forever. And if you truly love me, then its my request to please unlove me as soon as possible.
(With this line she left me over there and went away.)
That night I was unable to break down the meaning of her words. Even while returning to home in the evening I met with Siddharth and talked about it and he said he could interpret any of its mean. Every moment that was passing made my heart race faster. I was then feeling the same level of anxiety, sorrow and pain that was going on during the first days of love, when I hadn't become her friend.
The next day in the school when I met her, she left me with a smile and no talks were there that day. I t was really becoming terrible trauma for me. After the classes were over during the time of departure I tried to approach her. But she avoided. Such situation was there for around four to five days. I was literally feeling damn tensed about her changing behavior with me from the day I proposed her.
One day I purchased a burger for her as a surprise. During the hour, I made it reach to her by the help of her bestie Radhika. When she came to knew that I had given it for she had put on smile for me. She came to me and thanked.
I: Arey kya yaar. You are still sad with me.
She: Who said this that I'm sad with you. How could feel it yaar. Uss din bhi apse kaha tha we are never gonna break the friendship.
I:Then why don't you talk to me like earlier.

She: Its because you need some me time to think over the line that I had mentioned you.
I: If you don't mind then, can I ask you the reason of it.
She: Look if you are finding for the reason then I would like to make one thing completely clear that falling in love with me will never be worthy for you. I don't want my friend get spoiled just because of his emotion for me.
I: Ummm but....
Before I could say further, she left with eyes full of tear. I felt damn guilt for making her feel such sad due to me. I had never expected that my silly question would hurt her such! One thing I could make a note of, She was hiding something great which she hadn't disclose to me before. From that day we had just met each other just giving smile and no talks were initiated from both end.
One day, I found her to be absent. Radhika was present. I preffered to ask her.
I:Arey Radhika, Where's Shradha! Tum to janti ho ajkal who baat nhi karti. Is she okie or not?
Radhika just had eyes full of tear and with a heavy voice she wanted to say me something but couldn't control her tears rolling down her eyes.
I: Hey! What Happened....
Radhika: Before somedays bhai she denied to you to fall in love with her. Yeh she was right! Today the one who had always been her close intimate will have love for her to inifinity and wishes for her wellness.
I: Excuse me. I'm sry but actually I couldn't get your point.
Radhika: Bhai please if you have ever loved her truly then never let yourself cry today and will stand strong.
On hearing upon this line my body had shivered with anxiety and fear. The next moment what Radhika said me had led me to faint.......

# X

# The unexpected that broke me !!

When I opened up my eyes, Siddharth along with some teachers were surrounding me. I was bit unconscious of what was going on. Then I could recall what exactly had happened to me. As soon as I came back to my sense, I asked Siddharth to let me talk to Radhika. He replied, "No you can't meet her now. She had already left for the funeral". I was really stunned with the news.

Siddharth: Hey! Bhavesh here she left a message for you.

With this Siddharth handed over me a sheet of paper. I was shocked to see the handwriting of shradhanjali.

There she had written:

***"Hey Bhavesh!***

***How it all started in a sudden I don't know. The bonding we shared was always special and pious. I thank you for all the favour you had done to me. I guess you must have remember the day when you had donated your blood to save my life. Yeh I hadn't met any accident. Sry my dear, I was***

***suffering from leukaemia. I hadn't disclose this to ever in our friendship because I never wanted to have tears over the eyes of my close one's just because of me. You had also been the same special person for me like the way, I was for you. I will always be sry for treating you wrong at the last days, but believe me it was necessary. I know you will still be sad on me for what I did to you. Either it be ignoring you, hiding such truth to you and today for breaking my promise by not being with you forever. Yeh I hold the holy deity of Lord Shivji that you had presented me. Perhaps it was the best gift anyone would have ever given me in life. Will always be thankful for your love, care, affection, support and motivation. Yeh I know without my presence also you can do well. Never loose that spirit. I mayn't be with you physically, but I wish lord would allow me to be within you as your spirit to win. Before I would leave , promise me never to cry for me else I will not feel happy. As far I know you, you can never tolerate to see me anything less than smile. Lots of love and good wishes for the journey you would be going ahead. I'm sry my finger are numbing. Allow me to leave my dear.......***

***Yours Adorable,***

***Shradhanjali"***

After reading this letter, my heart was just shattered. I didn't blame lord or time for being such cruel to me but I cursed my fate for it. She took the promise from me not to cry. The greatest punishment I could get in my life for being in love. Siddharth then came back to me after few time. "Hey, let's get back. We are all asked to present in the class for mourning", he said.

Later that evening while returned home, I was filled with hopelessness. I was feeling as if, I had lost all of my happiness, strength, motivation and support. All I was left with tears, sorrow, hopelessness etc. That night I hadn't slept and was completely silence. Many a times mama tried to interacted with me to make myself free of these. It was in vain. The very next day, we were having our mock practice exam for boards. I was not ready at all. Somehow I managed to appear the paper. I remained silence for many days for this great change in my life. One day, I again opened up the same letter. I read it again. Yeh this time those lines had inspired me to pay her the real tribute. Yeh I loved he truly. I was meant to keep her smile wherever she would be. I promised myself that I wouldn't let her feel sad by proving myself a looser. From that day, I took the oath to secure top rank in the board. Finally, I made it with 97.8%. I still remember the day when I proudly hug her photo telling her "*I DID IT*".

***Some time we don't receive the love we expect it to be. They are meant to happen as destined by fate. Yes, we should never back out to give the best but still should have the courage to accept the uncertain terminating points. Love is the other name of freedom, strength, and courage until it become mixed up with expections.***

***No doubt, Shradhanjali and Bhavesh were meant for each other but time had chosen Arushi to be the better half of him. Here the true love for Shradhanjali had never diminished but it just have to be dumped into the corner of the heart. Sometime we can't blame anyone for what's going on in our life. It just happens as destined.***

***HAPPY ENDINGS :))))***

*After hearing the complete story, tears roll down from eyes of Arushi.*

*Bhavesh: Arushi I hope you wouldn't have judged me.*

*Arushi just burst out with tears and hugged Bhavesh. '*

*I can never do so. Infact after hearing all these even I feel proud of her. Its hard for all to feel their approaching end but still stand strong against it by putting on a smile. Really, in feel proud of you too that you truly meant her words and gave the real homage she asked for her life", Arushi said.*

*Bhavesh: I hope now you had got the reason of tears.*

*Arushi: Yeh I had. Don't worry, we will leave the life to the fullest. See we don't know what is the next. All we know is about the past and the present. It's better if don't over thin k about it.*

*The chirping sound of birds and the rays of morning sun had entered through the glass. Bhavesh said, "Arey kab subha hogaya kahani bolte bolte!"*

*Arushi I had a request.*

*Arushi: kya!*

*Bhavesh: Please close your eyes for some moments.*

*She then closed her eyes and Bhavesh with sudden blow of bursting noise of balloon had made her amazed. When she opened up her eyes. She was surprised with the cake before.*

*Bhavesh: HAPPY BIRTHDAY MY BAE.......*

*(Both of them hugged each other adorably.)*

Printed by Libri Plureos GmbH in Hamburg,
Germany